I DARE YOU

I DARE YOU

Jeff Ross

orca soundings

ORCA BOOK PUBLISHERS

Published in Canada and the United States in 2021 by Orca Book Publishers.
orcabook.com

Library and Archives Canada Cataloguing in Publication
Title: I dare you / Jeff Ross.
Names: Ross, Jeff, 1973- author.
Series: Orca soundings.
Description: Series statement: Orca soundings
Identifiers: Canadiana (print) 20210095423 | Canadiana (ebook) 2021009544X |
ISBN 9781459828018 (softcover) | ISBN 9781459828025 (PDF) |
ISBN 9781459828032 (EPUB)
Classification: LCC PS8635.O6928 I2 2021 | DDC jC813/.6—dc23

Library of Congress Control Number: 2020951469

Summary: In this high-interest accessible novel for teen readers, amateur filmmaker
Rainey has to deal with the aftermath of a prank gone wrong.

Orca Book Publishers is committed to reducing the consumption
of nonrenewable resources in the making of our books. We make
every effort to use materials that support a sustainable future.

Orca Book Publishers gratefully acknowledges the support for its
publishing programs provided by the following agencies: the Government
of Canada, the Canada Council for the Arts and the Province of British
Columbia through the BC Arts Council and the Book Publishing Tax Credit.

Edited by Tanya Trafford
Design by Ella Collier
Cover photography by GettyImages/Davil Wall (front) and
Shutterstock.com/Krasovski Dmitri (back)

Printed and bound in Canada.

24 23 22 21 • 1 2 3 4

To my parents

Chapter One

We thought it would be funny.

"Keep the camera low. Try to get the middle of people. No faces," Jordan said. "Make sure you get the school sign in a bunch."

I tilted the tiny screen so it was facing up, then held the camera low around my waist.

There were about fifty kids across the street, waiting for buses outside our town's only private high school.

"Remember the plan?" Jordan asked. I nodded, trying to keep my attention on the screen and not shift the angle. "Make sure once we start whaling on one another, you don't get our faces."

"If I do, I can fix it in post."

"Post?" Rowan said. "What the fuck's *post*?"

"Post-production. Like, where I'll edit the video and stuff."

Rowan looked annoyed by this.

"Better to get it out fast and make sure it looks real," Jordan said.

"It will," I said.

"Yeah, you're good at this shit, aren't you."

I checked the screen again.

"So I should punch you in the face, right?" Rowan said.

Rowan has one of those big round heads with a short tuft of hair on top. Jordan, on the other hand, is your regular square-jawed athletic type. Styled and stiff black hair. Bright blue eyes.

"No, don't fucking punch me in the face. Just make it *look* like you are."

"I'll try, but I ain't no stuntman."

As Jordan and Rowan walked down the block to cross the street, I moved into position. Jordan had handed me this camera an hour earlier, and I was still trying to figure out how everything worked.

The pickup area for the buses was crammed between the street and a brick-rimmed flower garden. This meant the fifty or so kids waiting for buses were packed in close to one another. So when Jordan and Rowan rolled into the middle of them, kids started tripping over one another trying to spread out. I moved, keeping the camera low and marking a time where the crowd was visible but what Jordan and Rowan were doing was out of frame.

I could start the video right at this spot when I began editing. As I moved closer, the garbled words of the kids became clearer. If anyone said anything clearly enough to be heard, I would make it more garbled. Before I even got to the curb, half a dozen kids had their phones up, filming. Jordan and Rowan were keeping it tight though. They kept pulling each other into headlocks and flailing around so their faces were always either down or turned to the weed garden.

"What the hell, guys!" A big dude wearing a tank top and shorts, even though it was just the beginning of spring, grabbed at Jordan and Rowan, trying, I guess, to separate them. Other than this one dude, though, no one else stepped in.

Sirens rattled the air. They were close. They likely didn't have anything to do with us, but it added to the drama. Jordan gave Rowan an extra bang in the stomach with his knee, shoved him away and took off running across the street. Rowan went down on the ground, then jumped up and ran along the sidewalk away from the school. The big guy took a couple of steps after Rowan, then stopped. I made sure I got the school's sign in the frame one last time before I shut off the camera and backed away. As I was crossing the street, I heard someone say, "Who the hell were those guys?"

I walked the block and a half to where we'd left Jordan's car and sat down on a bench. There were kids everywhere. Along with the high school, there was an elementary school just down the street. I hadn't been sitting for more than a minute before the lights flashed on Jordan's BMW and the doors unlocked. Without looking up, I opened the back passenger door and got in.

"Did you get it?" Jordan asked as he pulled away from the curb. He was breathing heavily, his face a bright red.

"Yeah, it'll look good."

He drove us two blocks north, turned left and there was Rowan, sitting on the bleachers of a ball diamond. Rowan swung off the bleachers and opened the passenger door before the car had come to a full stop.

“Did you get it?”

“I think it’ll look legit,” I said.

“What about our faces?”

“None as far as I could tell.” I’d already hooked up the camera to my laptop and transferred the file. I was scanning through the footage and hadn’t found any spots where you could clearly see Rowan or Jordan. They could be any two high-school kids.

“What about everyone with their cells?” Rowan asked.

“We’re two white guys outside a private school. That’s about as anonymous as you can get,” Jordan said with a laugh. “How fast can you get that up?”

“I’m working on it,” I said, slamming my teeth down on the repetition that was dying to come out. *Working on it, working on it, working on it.* I left it to ride in my mind, trying to push the words out by focusing more closely on the screen. They kept swirling, but I was determined not to tic out right then.

“Does it matter where we upload it from?” Jordan asked.

“No. I use a VPN.”

“Listen to this dark-web shit,” Rowan said.

“What’s that?”

“A virtual private network. It just means my location is hidden. It looks like I’m sending from somewhere in Alberta or whatever.” *Whatever, whatever, whatever.*

“So you can get it circulating in a bunch of places right away?”

“Yeah, it’s not going to take much editing.” I whistled and made that little grinding motion with my molars, and instantly I felt better. Evened out. If only for a moment. The radio was playing loudly enough that Jordan and Rowan could pretend they hadn’t heard me.

We pulled up outside a café, and I shut the lid on my laptop.

"You have the file on your computer?" Jordan asked.

"For sure," I said, and then that started circling. *For sure, for sure, for surrrrre.* I waved my hand a little, trying to calm my mind. To push away the desire to repeat those words. This whole situation was really heightening my anxiety, and when that happened I ticced out more.

"We'll take the camera back to Best Buy right now," Jordan said. I handed him the camera and he slid it into its box along with the transfer cable. "See you tomorrow, bruh. This is going to be awesome."

"You'll see it start circulating soon," I said.

"Take it easy, Rainman," Rowan said as I was closing the door.

Chapter Two

People call me Rainman partly because my name is Rainey and partly because of that old movie with Dustin Hoffman and Tom Cruise. I don't actually mind it. If nothing else, it gets the fact that I have Tourette's syndrome out in the open when I meet people. Someone introduces me as Rainman, and the new person will say, "Like in that movie?" And I get to explain that my name is Rainey and, yeah, kind of like the movie except the guy in the movie was autistic and I have Tourette's, which is totally different, but like the guy in the movie I'm a genius, and then we all laugh until I start ticcing out.

I wish I could stop having words and phrases rolling out of me all the time. I mean, I know I'm doing it. The words pop into my head and something tells me I have to get them out. I can sometimes hold them back for a while, but only for so long. When I was younger my parents made me go see psychiatrists and speech therapists. That went on for a few years, until they either got tired of bothering or figured it wasn't causing me any harm. I've never had swear words be a problem. Even when I tic out on the last word spoken, I don't end up swearing.

I don't mean that I don't ever swear. Sometimes I do. Who doesn't?

I have good friends. I get decent grades. And yeah, I'm embarrassed by it now and then. Would

I like it to go away? Sure. But then, who would I be without it?

I'm a sophomore now. I've been in school with Jordan since kindergarten, and we've always been friends. Rowan moved to our area a year ago, and the two of them became inseparable immediately. It might have been because of the wrestling team, or maybe they just hit it off. Who knows? I didn't feel threatened or anything, because that would be super weird.

The wrestling team was all I could think about with this whole fake fight scene. Then I looked it up, and wrestling season was over and William Fairfax Private School didn't even have a team. The only sport running was basketball, and it was still at the beginning of the season. Plus, the Fairfax team was in a completely different division. I could have asked Jordan what they were doing, I guess.

Maybe I should have.

I set my bag and computer down at an empty table and asked the woman sitting nearby to keep an eye on it. She gave me the nod we coffee-shop dwellers give one another. I went to the counter and ordered a decaf coffee. I don't know if caffeine affects my tics or not, but I decided ages ago not to risk things that aren't worth it. So regular coffee might taste better, but I'll never know.

Back at the table I settled in and quickly finished trimming the video. I made certain the beginning was abrupt. Like I was someone who'd just seen something and was fumbling with my phone. I watched the whole video without sound to make certain Jordan's and Rowan's faces never showed.

Then I listened without watching it, making sure I didn't hear anything but shouts and grunts and curses. Jordan said it had to seem like they were from Fairfax. So someone saying, "Who are these guys?" wouldn't work.

Finally I watched and listened to the video. It played really well. It looked like a cell-phone video, but there was something a little better about it. Like, I got the angles right, and the scuffle seemed way more violent than it had in reality. I set the editing program to render the video, then opened Hootsuite so I could post the video to all the different social media accounts I'd created over the previous year.

My interest in video started with one of those "What do you want to be when you grow up?" things at school. A bunch of people had come to our school to talk about various careers. Most of the kids weren't serious about it at all. They just went and hung out with the guy from the video-game company. There was a woman from a public-relations firm that focused on a client's online presence. Her talk was about how social media presence is everything these days. How traditional media is dying. How people don't watch TV or read newspapers. Everything is online, and it all needs to be delivered, discussed and dissected in real time. At the end of the talk, I kept asking her more questions.

When time ran out and she had to go, she said, "Honestly, what I like most about this job is how I can control a message. We really think about what goes out. Once the message is out there, it's our job to track it. We make certain that what we want to say and how we want it to be seen stays clear. If it starts to change, like if people alter our message somehow, or put up contrary opinions, we're ready to reinforce our message and set out to make *their* message look false." She got really juiced talking about all this and eventually, in quiet tones, admitted that every public-relations firm has numerous social media accounts under different names so messages can be bounced around. "It would take a lot of digging to prove that, though, so don't bother. And I never said this."

I was already into film, though living in Resurrection Falls, I wasn't confident I'd become a famous director someday. I just wanted to get better at filming and editing. But this whole controlling-the-message thing really grabbed me as well. I started creating different social media accounts just to see how hard it would be to do. I gave them each a different personality with their own pictures and avatars. Based on the type of person I'd created, I subscribed them to different groups and interests. I learned a ton about politics and sports. But mostly what I learned was how easily people get crazy about the stupidest things.

It was hilarious a lot of the time. I'd go into one of these discussion boards, put up an opposing view and then watch the carnage. It was pretty sad how easy it was to get people riled up.

So in the coffee shop that day, I set three accounts of fake local students to comment on how crazy the fight at Fairfax was. I had them asking if anyone had filmed it. I got the video up on a video channel, then released a slightly shorter version on a couple of other sites. After that I liked, commented on and tagged the video through several other accounts. Finally I used one of my "mom" accounts to post the video on a local moms' board, knowing it would get a lot of traction there.

Once everything was in motion, I went to the counter to get something to eat. I had to wait behind three people before I could order a cinnamon bun and refill my coffee. Back at my computer five minutes later, I checked in on my accounts. The number of likes and retweets was spinning. The numbers kept rising. I quickly scanned them. One early comment bothered me. **I'm a senior and don't know who these guys are.**

I went to one of my Fairfax accounts, logged in and replied, **You know everyone in the school? LOL!** I waited and watched.

A few seconds later the same person replied with **No, but I know a lot of ppl.**

Someone else wrote, **Isnt that Dylan or Devon? Grade 10? (I think).** I didn't reply to this. I just waited and, sure enough, someone else wrote, **Not Devon, but I think grade 10.** A few more replies popped up and then people started posting their own videos. I tagged all the ones where the guys' faces were fully obscured. Jordan and Rowan had really done a good job of keeping themselves turned so that no one could get a clear shot.

The videos were all the same. The same girl going, "Oh my god, what are they doing?" The same big guy coming in and grabbing at Jordan and Rowan. I mean, of course they were. This all really happened. Still, it was cool to see the different angles. I wondered what it would be like to put them together and make a full fight-scene film. I downloaded a bunch of them in case I wanted to try to piece that together someday for fun.

I waited until the first post had been liked over a hundred times and the video had more than fifty comments, then shut down my computer, finished my cinnamon roll and started to think about what we could do next.

Chapter Three

By that evening the video had gone viral. A local newscast played parts of it, connecting the fight with a growing "unease" among teens. The clip talked about how we, as teens, are disaffected, bored, unconnected and lost. Fighting in front of a school was happening because we wanted to feel *something.*

It was all bullshit, and hilarious, but I saw the look on my mom's face after she showed me the clip, and I decided not to laugh.

"Is this happening at your school?" she asked.

"Not that I've seen. But I pretty much keep my head down and mind my own business."

"So you haven't seen anyone fighting at the school?"

She looked so concerned. It was sad.

"That's the private school, right? Fairfax? One of the kids must have challenged the other to a trust-fund-off," I said. She didn't seem amused, although my dad laughed at that one. "No, honestly, kids mostly get along at my school. It's easier that way." This was mostly true. I mean, my school was like any school. There were little groups that hated on one another, individuals who got angry with other individuals for little or no reason. But it was mostly a peaceful place.

"If anything like that happens, you do something," Mom said.

"Like what?"

"Like that one boy tried to do in the video."

"That dump truck in a tank top? He stepped in and wasn't able to do anything. No, sorry, if a fight breaks out, I'm going to go ahead and leave those people alone."

"What if one of the boys doesn't want to be in a fight?" Mom asked.

Dad snorted.

She glared at him. "What?"

"What do you think it is, hon, a fight club? These guys get angry at one another for some reason. Likely a girl. And they hit one another. It's been happening since caveman time, and I doubt it's going to change now."

"But what if the boy is being bullied?" Mom said.

And I hadn't even said it, but the words started swirling. "Beingbullied, beingbullied, beingbullied."

Mom looked at Dad. Dad looked at Mom.

"Well," Mom said over top of me, "I think it's stupid and pointless."

"Exactly!" Dad said. "As it was, it shall always be."

Jordan's BMW was parked a few doors down from my house when I returned from school the next day. I walked up, opened the door and slid in.

"That video was awesome," he said. He was wearing a baseball cap and dark glasses, as though he was undercover. "It was on the news. Did you see it?"

"Yeah, my mom showed it to me last night."

"You didn't say you had anything to do with it, did you?"

"Hells no," I said. A woman walking her dog passed us. My mind said, *Dogs bark. They go wuff, wuff, wuff. You should go wuff, wuff, wuff at the dog.* I pushed the necessity down and nodded my head a bunch.

"I got another one," Jordan said.

"Another what?"

"Video idea."

"What was that last one all about?"

"What do you mean?" Jordan kept looking at his face in the rearview mirror, then picking at something beside his nose.

"Why get into a fight outside that school?"

"Oh, some dirtbag from there stole Row's girl."

I've always hated that phrase. *Stole his girl.* Like she was a possession that could be taken away. My guess was this girl decided not to date Rowan, or she had dated him and didn't want to anymore. Either way, it was her choice.

"Ah, okay," I said. "So what did that fake fight do?"

"The girl's parents are super protective. I guess he figured they'd see it and she wouldn't be allowed out anymore."

"Posting to that moms' board makes way more sense now. Did it work?"

"Fuck if I know. Who cares?"

I shrugged. I guessed it didn't matter. "So what's the next idea?"

Jordan took his glasses off and looked straight at me. He looked like the kid I used to hang out with all the time. His eyes were bright, and his lips curled just so.

"Okay, here's what I want to do. We get something circulating about—like, this girl. Like, a ghostly girl coming out of the forest."

I gave him a look. My mind said, *Woof, woof, woof.*

"Would anyone fall for that?"

"For sure. People are stupid, man."

"That's true. Where are we going to get a little girl?" I paused as the woofing built inside my head. Then I laughed/barked. "That sounds bad."

"Yeah, you're right. Okay, like, a dude then. A hitchhiker coming out of the woods. That's creepy in a different way."

I was already thinking of places where we could film. Angles that would make things more creepy. Lighting. Something to make it all seem eerie yet real.

"Will we eventually say it was us?" I asked. For some reason this mattered to me. I wanted to get credit for this if it worked. It could be my calling card for a social media or film job.

"Eventually, yeah. Sure. To show people they shouldn't be so stupid and believe everything that shows up on social media."

"Do you think we'd get in trouble?"

Jordan gave me a look that triggered something inside me that wanted to tic out. The *woof, woof, woof* was burning the back of my throat. I needed to do it—I needed to bark.

"From who?"

"Police?" I squeaked.

"No," he said. "Not a chance. What could happen that would get us in trouble? It'll just be a video. Are you in?"

I closed my eyes and tried to push the tic away. But it wasn't going anywhere.

"I'm in," I said, then opened the door and jumped out. "Talk soon."

The second Jordan pulled away from the curb, I started barking. I tried to muffle it, but that made my head twitch and my hands shake. So I let it go. I was full-out barking in the street. The dog was gone. Everyone was gone. I was barking at an empty street. Before the black BMW had turned the corner at the end of my block, it was over, and I felt much better. I felt absolutely fine.

Chapter Four

After final class the following day, Jordan, Rowan and I went to the art room. Mrs. Cain was there, but she was always happy to believe students were taking an interest in her class. She was also super suspicious of anyone at school after hours. Jordan and I were both in her art class, but she had no idea who Rowan was.

"He's here to help fit the sheets together for my project," Jordan said before he could be asked.

"The plywood?"

"Yeah. I want to test that the thing is going to hold before I go any further."

"Okay," she said, though she still sounded super suspicious. "Be careful, don't destroy the place, and tidy up when you're done."

"For sure," Jordan said. Before she was even out the door, he'd started pulling the sheets of plywood from behind a cabinet.

"What is that even?" I asked.

"I'm going to throw some paint on it and call it art," Jordan said. "I really just wanted to make the biggest thing I could." The supply cabinets were massive and filled with materials. Some of it was pure junk. And most of the kids loved digging around in it. Taking found things and calling it art was huge for anyone who couldn't draw. But we weren't there for the junk. We were there for the fabrics.

When Jordan had come up with his idea, I'd remembered seeing this long cape-like thing in the supply cupboard. At first I'd thought it was a Halloween costume, but when I'd gotten a closer look, I'd recognized it for what it was—a huge sheet with a hole in it. With a couple of safety pins to make it tighter, I imagined it would look really creepy.

"What is it we're doing here?" Rowan asked.

"I told you, Row," Jordan said.

Rowan was combing through the materials, knocking stuff onto the floor and not bothering to put any of it back. "Tell me again."

"We're going to do a kind of Slender Man or Momo thing. This figure is going to come out of the woods, and we'll film it. When it goes up online, it'll go viral."

"Viral," Rowan said. "Why would you even care?"

"It'll be everywhere," I said.

"Online," Rowan said.

"Yes, online, Row." Jordan stopped what he was doing and looked at his friend. "You really don't do anything online, do you?"

"Never seen the use. Seems like a waste of time."

"Well, this is going to freak people out. We'll put a story around it as well."

"Sounds dumb," Rowan said. "And exactly why I don't spend my time on there. If idiots like you two can get a whole bunch of people freaked out about nothing, what's the point?"

"It's funny," Jordan said. "Anyway, you don't have to make the outfit or anything."

"So why am I here?"

"You're the one coming out of the woods."

"No fucking way," Rowan said.

"We already talked about this, Row. You'll just stumble out onto the road, then go back into the woods. That's it. I'll be driving along the road, and Rainey'll film it."

"Why would I want to do this?"

"It'll be hilarious," Jordan said. He'd found a fake ax and was swinging it at Rowan's legs, pretending to chop him down.

"It's fucking dumb."

"Come on, man. I dare you."

"Yeah, I dare you," I said.

"Ohhh, the two of you *dare* me. Well, I guess I have to do it or I'll look like a *wimp* then."

"There you go," Jordan said, shaking his head in what I guessed was disgust as soon as Rowan had turned his back. "That could be part of the video too. Like, we tell people we dare them to try and find the thing, whatever we call it."

"A figure coming out of the woods *and* a challenge," I said. My mind was exploding with the potential.

"This is going to be insane."

"Here it is," I said, grabbing the long sheet. Even with me holding it at arm's length above my head, it touched the floor. It was thin enough that it would waver in a breeze, but not so thin that you'd be able to see Rowan's form beneath it. The hole in the top wasn't quite big enough for Rowan's head, so I carefully made it larger. The problem that immediately emerged was Rowan now looked like a blob. Blobs aren't frightening. We got him to move, and he continued to look like a blob with a head.

"Here," Jordan said, thrusting a couple of Halloween brooms at Rowan. "Hold on to these." The brooms gave his body a bit of definition. They looked like arms, at least a little, and because of their length, his body seemed really long. I grabbed some safety pins and fit them around his arms. If I left it alone he'd just look like a big ghost. But with the safety pins I was able to pull the material closer to his body and keep it there. Now he was beginning to look like a thing. When he moved, the fabric kind of fluttered around him. It was long enough that it fell just above his ankles. His movements seemed more like he was floating than walking.

"This is good," I said. "But we need to do something about his head."

"I should do something about your head," Rowan said. But he wasn't serious. He was in front of the full-length mirror, checking himself out.

"Either bigger or make it disappear," Jordan said.

"Like a pumpkin, or just bring the material up higher?" I asked.

Jordan was rummaging through a cupboard. "Not a pumpkin. But also not like Slender Man. No hat or anything." He pulled out a tall foam triangle. It was bendable. I wondered what the hell it was supposed to be and who'd made it.

"Try this," he said.

"Where?" Rowan replied.

"On your head."

"I won't be able to fucking see."

"We'll cut holes if we need to. Let's just see if it works."

Rowan reluctantly put the triangle on his head. I pulled the material up about halfway and secured it with safety pins. This left his calves exposed. I got on a stool and grabbed the top of the triangle and bent it back slightly. Not a lot, just enough to give the whole thing a shape that looked like it could be human but not quite.

"That's it," Jordan said. He ran and closed the classroom door. "Walk across the room and back." The blinds were shut on the windows, leaving only the sputtering fluorescent bulbs for light.

"Shut those lights off," I said.

Jordan turned the lights off, and we were thrown into darkness. I switched on two lights Mrs. Cain kept in the corner, the kind you'd see onstage at a concert. I pointed them both at the ceiling and then turned on a large fan. The lights flickered as they warmed, and as Rowan walked, the breeze from the fan caught the fabric and made it ripple. I couldn't think of a better look. It was creepy as hell. He looked humanlike—this wasn't some kind of bear or

Sasquatch thing—but at the same time he didn't look human at all.

Rowan raised the brooms and made a moaning sound.

"No, none of that," Jordan said. "That just looks creepy."

"Isn't that what we're going for?"

"Yeah, but it looks like someone *trying* to look creepy. Just move. Shift the brooms a little as you go. But not much. And go slowly. So it kind of seems like your feet are moving but maybe not."

"Exactly," I said. "It all has to look right but not quite right."

"What is this, Hamlet?" Rowan said. But he walked. And it was perfect. I knew what was going on—I mean, I'd helped create it. But as he came across the room, I was totally freaked out. It didn't seem normal.

Which was exactly what we were looking for.

"Okay, get it off," Jordan said as he flicked the lights back on. He moved to the step to remove the triangle. "Before someone comes in." He looked at me. His eyes were shining. "This is going to be awesome."

And I had to agree.

Chapter Five

We decided to film that night. I borrowed the lights from the art room, and Jordan bought a camera from a different Best Buy. I got to the woods first and looked for spots to set up the lights. My Social Sciences book fell out of the back seat of my mom's car when I pulled out a light. I'd told my parents I was going to study, and they had believed me, and I felt awful about that. I didn't want to lie to them, but I couldn't tell them I was going to the woods to film a video. First of all, they wouldn't have let me. And secondly, they would have known then about our idea.

No one could know. That was the point.

I'd brought battery packs for the lights. They had maybe half an hour of power in them. I moved the lights around in the woods, seeing what they looked like from the road. There needed to be a bit of light, so we could actually see Rowan coming onto the road, but not so much that the scene looked lit. It was a delicate balance.

Even though I was busy setting up lights and knew there was nothing freaky about the woods, I did get a little scared. Every so often I'd hear a noise—the snapping of a twig or an owl hooting—and I'd get a shiver up my back.

In the time I'd been here, only one other vehicle had gone by. I was pretty relieved when Jordan and Rowan pulled up.

"Won't that look fake?" Rowan asked as he swung out of the car.

"We need a glow so the camera can see you," I said. I brought Rowan and Jordan to the other side of the road and held up my phone with the camera on. "See, it looks like something is going on in there, but what exactly it is, you can't really tell." They both looked at my phone and then back at the woods.

"That's weird." Jordan handed me the camera.

"I don't think I want to use that," I said.

"Why not?"

"Because it will be too clear a picture." I pulled another phone from my pocket. "This one will be way better."

"That old piece of shit?" Rowan said.

It was an iPhone 6. The camera on those was good for the time, but not great in dim light.

"It'll be perfect if we film from the car."

"What?" Jordan said.

"Well, we can't just happen to be out here walking on the road and then spot this thing coming out of the woods. My idea is that Rowan gets in the woods, he walks toward the road, and I film from inside the car. You can say, 'Seriously, what the hell is that?' or something, and that's what the video starts with. Then we swerve so the headlights aren't on him, and he'll stop and turn back into the woods. If we keep our distance, say"—I walked back a little and turned again—"here, there will never be a clear shot of him. I can keep it out of frame a bit as well."

Jordan was nodding to this. "Yeah, I can see that working, yeah."

A bit of lightning flashed in the distance, and then we heard a low rumble. That would add to the atmosphere. But I wasn't sure I wanted it any closer. "Get in your shit."

"I still don't get why you two want to do this," Rowan said.

"People are idiots," Jordan said.

"Okay. And?"

"I want—*we* want to expose that. Like, these idiots will believe anything they see online. I'm thinking of using this as my senior paper."

"A senior paper on how you duped people online?" Rowan said.

"Yeah. I want to get into advertising. It would be perfect."

"Why are *you* doing this?" Rowan asked me.

And for some reason, that set off a bunch of tics. I whistled and shook my head a couple of times before I could answer. Rowan stared at me the way people do when I tic out and they're not used to it. Like he was freaked out by it but at the same time pretending it wasn't happening.

"I want to get into film and public relations," I said. "It's all practice."

"And what am *I* getting out of this?"

"You're the star," Jordan said, giving Rowan a pat on the back and leading him toward his car. "Now let's get you suited up."

"Before the rain comes."

"We only have about twenty minutes before the batteries die on the lights," I said. "Maybe two takes."

"We'll nail this in one," Jordan said as he opened his trunk. We got Rowan dressed quickly. I'd parked my mom's car in a lane, and Jordan had pulled over in a little picnic spot. But we wouldn't even have needed to bother. Not a single car passed as we got Rowan ready.

I took Rowan to a starting place, and he put an earbud in one ear. I tilted the triangle as a breeze pushed through the leaves. I will tell you this—it was creepy as hell.

"What?" Rowan said.

"That's so creepy," I said.

"That's what you wanted, right?"

"Yeah," I said. I brought my phone out. "Answer this," I said as I called him.

"Got it," he said, his voice coming through the phone and right in front of me at once.

"Dude, this is so creepy," I said.

"Just hurry up. Before someone drives by."

I ran back to the road and got into Jordan's car.

"You still hear me?" I said into my phone.

"I'm still on the phone. So yeah, I can hear you."

"What are we doing?" Jordan asked.

"Drive back up the road a bit, and turn around."

I got my old phone out. I'd done a factory reset so there wouldn't be any personal information stored. I'd strip anything from it before posting anyway. "Then I'll get Rowan to start walking. When he comes out of the woods, slow down and steer away from him. Try not to hit him dead-on with your headlights."

As Jordan was turning the car around, he said, "I can see the lights in the woods."

"You won't in the video. Forget what you can see right now."

Jordan turned a perfect one-eighty about half a mile from where we'd been.

"Try and get up to a regular speed. So when we get close you'll have to hit the brakes a little."

"Should I slide out?"

"A little." I had the old iPhone up in front of me. I'd edit the video before I posted it, so I decided to start filming right away. I rested one arm on the dashboard so there'd be a bit of sway to the video. It was so dark that the only things visible were directly in front of the headlights. "Okay. In five seconds say, 'What's that?' Rowan, start walking. Five, four, three, two, one."

"What's that?" Jordan's voice cracked.

Perfect.

Rowan shuffled out of the woods at exactly the right moment. Jordan hit the brakes—harder than I'd expected. The phone fell from my hands. I picked it up as it slid toward me. Jordan was steering the car sideways. The headlights were all over the place. I got the phone back in position and caught Rowan as he was slipping back into the woods. I managed to hold the phone directly on him for a moment. There was a flash of lightning in the distance.

Jordan threw an arm over his mouth and said, "What is that thing?" Exhaust drifted past the headlights. I could just make out Rowan moving through the trees. All he was doing was walking. One foot in front of the other, moving around the trees. But it looked eerie. As though he was floating.

I shut the video down and looked over at Jordan.

"That was perfect," I said.

"Holy shit, that was awesome."

"Are we done?" Rowan asked.

"One second. Stay there. In case we need another take." I flicked through the video as quickly as possible. It looked great. It was hard to be certain, but it seemed like it would work. "I think it's good."

"You sure?" Jordan asked.

"No. But we should leave before someone spots us out here. If we have to come back, we have to come back."

"Yeah. Okay. Rowan, you still there?"

"Where the fuck would I go?"

"Go to my car," I said. "It's, like, twenty feet from you." We could hear Rowan shuffling around.

"Where...oh, forget it. I see it."

I put my phones in my pockets. "Drop me up there," I said. "I'll take Rowan home."

"This is so awesome," Jordan said.

"Awesome, awesome, awesome, awesome," I said, and I wasn't even ticcing out.

Chapter Six

Two days later the video was everywhere. It took so little to get it started, but once something like that *is* started, it's hard to stop it. I countered a lot of the "It's fake" messages with "Looks pretty real to me." That's the thing about people—they want to believe. It might be stupid to believe, and what they're seeing might defy explanation, but they want to believe.

"They think it's real because they're idiots," Jordan said.

I didn't want to think that, but it was hard not to. My mom thought it was real. Or, at least, she said she found it "odd." Dad thought it was some creep who likely lived in the woods. When online news picked up on it, people started tearing the video apart. Looking for hints of where it was shot. I was pleased I'd stripped away the identifying information. It didn't take long, though, for some internet detectives to figure out it had to be in our area.

The lightning was the first clue. Someone spotted it in the video and then searched out all the places in the world where lightning had occurred that night. We should have put a different story on the video, I thought. Instead of *THIS came out of the woods at us last night*, I should have done an *I caught this a bit ago and have been too afraid to share*. The internet detectives' next step, apparently, would be looking at the vegetation, the side of the road we were driving on, the rocks and then the yield sign in the distance.

I hadn't even noticed the sign.

It was nothing more exciting than a yield sign, but apparently was clearly American in style.

Within two days our general area had been targeted.

"It's fine," Jordan said.

But I was worried. Especially since we'd added *I dare you to find this thing yourself.* The last thing we needed was people combing our area, looking for some weird *thing* in the woods.

"There are some people who are really serious about this shit," I said.

"What do you mean?"

"They investigate it. They need to know. They want to debunk these types of things. Or prove they're true."

Jordan's smile grew. "Perfect! They can duke it out."

Someone dropped a plate of dishes in the kitchen of the coffee shop. The place went quiet for a minute before someone clapped, someone asked if everything was all right, and then we all went back to our individual conversations. "What are you worried about?"

"Nothing, I guess."

"Good, because we're going to do another one right away."

"What? Why?"

"We need to give some ammunition to the believers." He pointed at my screen, which showed that the number of views continued to climb. We were on the cusp of making money from it. The problem was, I'd used a fake email and name to put it up. I was certain there were ways to hide who you were and still get paid. But having seen the way people were investigating every aspect of the video, I couldn't imagine getting away with it.

"You want to make a new video?"

"One more. Then we move on to something else." Jordan was shaking his head at the screen.

"What?"

"Idiots," he said. "Gullible idiots. A boogeyman coming out of the woods. Yeah, for sure, that's real." He kept shaking his head.

I'd enjoyed making the video and was amazed at how many people believed what they saw. But I was beginning to feel as though Jordan and I were in this for totally different reasons.

"Some people just question things," I said. "Like, they glance at the video and think *maybe*."

"Yeah, which is stupid. Like, give it a second of thought. Anyway."

"Is Rowan into doing another video?"

"Yeah, I'll get him to do it. Let's go tonight, before anyone actually figures out the location."

"Same spot?"

“May as well. Keep it authentic.” Jordan downed his coffee and stood. “You want a real camera or just use that iPhone again?”

“Let’s get a real camera. Then we can do it like we were waiting out there. You know? We found the location and filmed the thing.” My mind was racing again. “I can make a new account for it. Someone who says he wants to keep this thing to himself. But then we’re done with it, right?”

“I’m done if you’re done,” Jordan said.

The words swirled. They ached in my brain. I’d been trying to control the tics lately, even though I knew I just needed to let them flow. The longer I kept the swirling feeling inside, the longer each tic lasted.

I gave two whistles, a head shake and a flip with my left hand, and it was gone. Like a wave slightly bigger than all the other waves inside my brain had rolled up and then washed itself out on the beach.

"We can do something else after this," I said. "Something legit."

"Sure," Jordan said. "Why not? I'll pick you up at eight."

"Cool," I said. Then, as Jordan walked away, "Cool cool cool cool cool."

Chapter Seven

Using a real camera would make a difference. It would be higher quality, but I'd also be able to work with it more in the editing software. I also had to be that much more careful. We decided to take a more investigative approach. Jordan would do the talking and be in the video, but he would never turn around. The camera was full HD and had a mounted light. I dialed the light back so it wasn't fully on but still made the area glow. We were lucky—the rain had passed and the sky was cloudless. A big moon sat low behind us.

“You ready, Rowan?” I asked.

“This is the last time,” Rowan replied. “Stumbling around in the stupid woods.”

“Are you ready?”

“Yes, fuck.”

I turned the camera on and angled it low enough to keep Jordan’s head mostly out of the frame.

“Go.”

Jordan began walking, looking at the ground. “It was around here that I saw the markings. They weren’t, like, footprints. Just...I don’t know, *drag* marks?” He turned his head slightly. Almost enough to show a full profile, but stopping just short. He looked back down, scuffed the ground with his foot. He’d put on a pair of his dad’s tasseled shoes.

We were doing this without the lights in the woods, so when Rowan came out, it would be from complete darkness.

"I thought this might be the right spot," Jordan said. "From that other video. I've driven here before, and the sign and the bend in the road—it just seemed right." He cut into the shallow ditch, and we moved along the edge of the forest. The idea was that Rowan would come out far away, Jordan would spot him, and we'd run toward him.

I coughed into my mic, the signal for Rowan to emerge. I kept the camera low but slowly raised it.

"I mean, it could be anything. Like, an owl caught a rabbit and dragged it out here. But the marks go deeper into the woods. I was going to follow them earlier when I was here, but I didn't want anyone to see me." He turned his head slightly as I had the camera roam up and over. I could see Rowan in the upper corner of the frame. But Jordan hadn't seen him yet. Or was making like he hadn't.

"There were also the marks farther down." Jordan raised his head as Rowan stepped onto the road. "Holy shit, there it is." Jordan didn't run right away.

Who would? He stood there frozen for a moment. Then he said, "We have to get closer."

He started to run.

And then the area around Rowan was brighter. At first I was confused. I hadn't set any lights, so it wasn't coming from us. And the camera's light wouldn't go that far. Rowan was on the side of the road, and I could see him turning his head away from us. Jordan was still running, stumbling as he tried to climb back onto the road. The lights got brighter, illuminating the entire area. And then the car appeared.

At first it seemed as though it would just drive past. Then the headlights fully hit Rowan, and the driver steered hard, putting the car into a slide. Rowan jumped into the ditch as the back of the car sliced past him. Jordan and I did the same, although we were far enough away that we weren't in any danger. The car spun, went up on two wheels, hit something and rolled.

"Holy shit," Jordan said. The car rolled twice, then slammed into a tree on the other side of the road and lay there, upside down, smoking.

The silence after all the noise of the screeching tires and crumpling metal was deafening.

At first I thought Rowan was running toward the car. But he didn't cross the road. He was trying to pull the triangle off his head. He had the fabric pulled up around his waist. He looked like a nun in a marathon.

He came to a sliding stop beside us. "Let's get the hell out of here."

"What?" I said. "We have to see if the driver is okay."

"I am not sticking around here," Rowan said. He'd managed to get the triangle off and, without another word, was running toward Jordan's car.

Jordan looked at me for a moment. Then he reached out and grabbed the camera.

"We can't be here," he said.

"We have to see if the driver is okay," I said.

"No way." I looked at the car and couldn't see any movement from the driver.

Jordan was already a few steps away from me. "Come on."

"We have to help."

Jordan raised his arms and shrugged. Then he ran to his car. Ten seconds later I was standing out there alone.

I ran to the car. It was a black Ford, and someone inside was talking. It sounded like there were multiple people inside, but then I recognized the tinny sound of a voice coming through a small speaker.

"Mrs. Calder, can you hear me?" the voice asked.

The woman was upside down, restrained by her seat belt. She looked at me when I crouched beside the car.

"Mrs. Calder, help is on its way," the voice continued. "If you could tell me what happened..."

Her mouth was moving like she was a fish out of water. The windscreen was shattered and dangling in front of her. The airbag had exploded and was hanging limply from the steering wheel.

Her eyes were huge and bright and staring at me.

"Are you okay?" I asked.

"Who's that?" the voice on the speaker asked. "May I ask your name? Were you in the vehicle?"

"No, I wasn't. I was out here."

The woman's mouth kept opening and closing. A trickle of blood dripped onto the ceiling from her forehead.

"Can you tell me the condition of Mrs. Calder? Is she breathing?"

I put my hand in front of the woman's face, even though I could clearly see that she was breathing.

"Yes, she is."

"Is she conscious?"

"Yes."

"Can you tell me why she is not responding?"

The woman's eyes closed, then slowly opened again.

"I think she banged her head."

"An ambulance has been called and is on its way. Do you hear the sirens?"

I leaned out of the car, and the sharp smell of gasoline hit me.

"Is there a chance the car could blow up?" I yelled. I could hear a siren in the distance. I couldn't tell how far away it was or which direction it was coming from.

"Do you smell gasoline?"

"Yes."

"Is the car running?"

For some reason it took me a moment to answer this. "No, it stalled out."

"I don't want you to move her, but there is a slim chance that the car might combust. One moment."

The voice disappeared, and I had never felt so alone. The woman's mouth had stopped opening and closing, and she looked like a bat, eyes closed, upside down. Her hair lay across the ceiling. She looked to be in her forties. Or younger. It was hard to tell.

"You're going to be okay," I said. I thought she nodded. It was hard to tell.

"Sir," the voice came again.

"What?"

"I believe you should see an ambulance in a moment. Or a paramedic truck."

I looked away from the car again just as the woods were illuminated by headlights.

"I do."

"They will take over. But please, until they arrive, stay with Mrs. Calder. You have been very helpful."

The ambulance stopped right next to the car and two men jumped out, pulling on gloves.

"What's the situation here?" one of them asked. There were more sirens. A fire truck turned the bend, its siren wailing.

"Her car flipped, and she seems awake but isn't talking."

"Hello, I'm Natalie from Roadside Assistance," said the voice on the speaker. "Who am I talking to?"

I backed away from the window so the paramedic could get closer.

"This is Richard."

I bumped into the other paramedic as I moved backward.

"Whoa there. You all right, kid?" he asked.

"Yeah," I said. "Yeah, I'm fine."

"How'd you get out of the car?"

"I wasn't in it."

The paramedic looked around, then back at me. "Where's your car?"

"I don't have one."

He turned his head slightly sideways. "Where'd you come from?"

"Hey, Jared," Richard said from beside the car. "Hold her while I cut this seat belt."

Jared bent down and reached into the car. He angled himself so he could support the woman.

The fire truck had come to a halt, and men were exiting it. No police had shown up yet, and I knew I could run. I could just run and get out of there. It would be a hike, but I could make it home in an hour.

But I didn't. I just stood there. For what felt like forever.

Chapter Eight

When the police got around to questioning me, I lied, but first of all, I'm not very good at it, and secondly, my lie was super unconvincing. I'd been running, I said. At night, on a road in the middle of nowhere, in jeans.

Even to me it sounded totally stupid, but I just couldn't come up with anything else.

The police were busy dealing with the crime scene for a while, so I sat in the back of the cruiser and tried to figure out what other stories I could tell. The only thing close was that I had seen the video online, thought I recognized the place and gone to investigate. But still, it was an hour from my house, and I didn't have a car. The problem with any kind of lie, though, is that you have to stick with it. I couldn't suddenly give them something else. And I'd be admitting I was a moron who'd been duped by some stupid video. I couldn't bring myself to do that.

Meanwhile, my phone kept binging with text messages from Jordan. They were weird: **Hey, what are you up to tonight? Hit me back if yer bored.**

When the cops, two of them, returned to the cruiser, they seemed to forget I was there. We drove for a while as they talked about how the accident could have been much worse and speculated on what had happened to the woman's ability to speak.

"Is she going to be okay?" I asked.

"That depends on what okay looks like to you, I'd say," the male officer said. The female officer just glanced at me as she drove.

"I mean, like, she's going to live, right?"

"She'll live," the male officer said. He turned to me, then looked at something on his nails. The cruiser was well lit from the computer and all the stuff on the dashboard. "What were you doing out there?"

"Running," I said, because I felt I had to dig in. And then that stuck in my head and swirled. *You run, you're a runner, run, run, run*. I let that slide out of me in a stream of whistles and yelps, which turned the officer back around.

They put me in a conference room to wait for my parents to arrive. I guess I was a bit of a problem. Like, what could they do with me? As far as I knew, the woman in the accident hadn't spoken yet. I decided I had to lock on to my lie. It was a stupid lie and I knew it, but it was all I had. I could alter it a little if I had to.

I could say I'd gone out there because it was where I thought the video had been filmed. But that would only be if the video ever came up. Or if the woman began talking and spoke about what she'd seen.

I decided I'd try to keep myself flexible. Be ready to pivot, as they say in public relations.

The two officers came into the conference room and sat down.

"I don't think we introduced ourselves before," the woman said. "I'm Detective Carol Evans, and this is Officer Jeff Cain." Officer Cain removed his hat and set it on the table.

"Hi," I said.

"How old are you, Rainey?"

"He's sixteen," Officer Cain said. He kind of winked at me. "He's in my wife's art class."

This left me feeling embarrassed. Because for sure he would tell Mrs. Cain. And on top of that, I suddenly thought, she might connect me to the fabric we'd put on Rowan. That's the problem with living in a smallish town—everyone knows everyone else's business.

"Ahh, okay. Well, we cannot legally ask you any questions until your parents arrive. Would you like a drink or something to eat?"

"I'd like to go home."

"And you will, soon enough."

"I'll have a Sprite or whatever," I said.

They stood as one and left the room. The next time the door opened, my parents were standing there. And if I were to tell you I had no idea what disappointment looked like before that moment, you'd have to believe me. Mom looked like she was going to cry, and Dad, for the first time ever, looked like he might actually hit something.

"What is this all about?" Dad asked. He and Mom stepped in, followed by Detective Evans and Officer Cain.

"Would you like to take a seat?" Detective Evans said. My parents swung around the table and sat down on either side of me. You'd think that would have made me feel better, but it only made me feel worse. Like I'd done this stupid thing and now they'd been dragged into it.

"I understand you don't have a lot of information regarding what occurred this evening."

"We know our son is in the police station," Dad said angrily.

Mom whimpered.

"There was an accident tonight on Clover Side Road. Do you know it?"

"Sure," Dad said.

"A vehicle driven by a young woman rolled and crashed. There were no other vehicles involved. When first responders arrived, Rainey was attempting to help the woman."

"What was he doing out there?"

"That's the question we have as well."

And just like that, everyone was looking at me. And I had no idea what to say. So I stuck to my lie. Which was, of course, preceded by a ten-second tic fest. Everyone watched me go through this until I started talking.

"I was out for a run." This made Mom look even sadder.

"I see," Detective Evans said. "We do have some issues with that statement. First of all, you're wearing jeans. Secondly, Clover Side Road is not near any other roads one might run on. In fact, it's a dead end since the bridge washed out. And thirdly, it was dark out. None of these really add up to a good run."

I decided not to say anything.

"Tell us the truth, Rainey," Dad said. "What were you doing out there?"

I looked at the table. I kept looking at it until Officer Cain said, "Well, we can't keep him here. As far as we know, no crime has been committed. The woman in the accident was pretty banged up and is currently nonverbal. We'll have to wait to see how she is."

"Are there going to be charges?" Mom asked, her voice totally falling apart in the process.

"Right now," Detective Evans said, leaning forward, "we have a single-car accident. That's all. Your son's presence at the scene is strange though. We'd like to know why he was there."

"Running," I said. Totally locked in. "I was out running."

Bruh where are you?

Seriously

WTF

Bruh?

There were twenty of these messages on my phone when I finally looked at it. I'd felt it vibrating in my pocket but hadn't wanted to pull it out. They were all from Jordan.

I read through them twice and realized something—he hadn't mentioned that we'd been together. I scanned through earlier texts, and there was nothing about the videos there either. Everything he and I had planned, we'd talked about in person.

I didn't know whether this was on purpose or not. It wasn't from my end but could have been from his.

I lay in my bed that night staring at the ceiling and convincing myself this would all go away soon enough. The woman would be fine but not remember anything. There'd be this hour-long blank in her memory, and she'd have no idea why she had crashed her car. Officer Cain wouldn't talk to his wife about finding me out on that empty road. Because if he did, she would start to wonder why I was there. And then she'd start thinking about how strange it was that for the *first time ever,* Jordan, Rowan and I had been in her classroom after school hours. If I could have made that video go away, I would have. But it had caught some serious traction and been shared all over the world.

I'd done too good a job.

I decided not to answer Jordan. I'd see him at school the next day anyway. And although I found it hard to go to sleep, eventually I did.

Chapter Nine

"Dude, what the fuck?" Jordan grabbed me as I was walking into the school and swung me into the entryway to the maintenance room. "What happened?"

"That woman was messed up," I said.

"Is she dead?"

"I don't think so."

He let go of my shirt. "Why didn't you leave with us?"

"I had to see if she was okay," I said. "I mean, we caused her to crash."

"No we didn't," Jordan said. "She was likely out there looking for the boogeyman."

"If so, then we're to blame," I said. Kids were looking at us as they walked down the hall. I'd had a horrible night and woken up certain I'd been part of ruining a woman's life.

"No, her being an idiot is to blame. A gullible moron."

"Do you believe that?"

"If she was out there looking for the triangle-headed man, then yeah, I do."

"What if she wasn't? What if she was just driving out there?"

"Then she made a choice to totally overreact and flip her car. Either way, none of this is on us." He backed away. "You're not going to say anything, are you?"

"No," I said. Because I figured it wouldn't matter. What had happened had happened. I just hoped the woman was okay.

"Good."

"I think I'm done with those kinds of videos though," I said.

"Oh yeah, for sure. Me too." Jordan melded into the crowd of people heading to class. I straightened my shirt and did the same.

Mrs. Cain looked at me oddly in art class. Or maybe I was just imagining it. Either way, I spent the entire time ticcing out and leaving to "go to the bathroom."

At the end of class, Mrs. Cain stopped me.

"Rainey, can I have a quick word?"

I stood there as my classmates swept past. "Sure," I said.

"I heard what happened last night. Are you okay?"

I nodded a whole bunch because my mind was telling me to keep nodding until I could twist my head to one side. Once I'd managed to do that, I stared at Mrs. Cain.

"I have to ask, why were you out there?"

"Running."

She gave me the saddest smile.

"You're not on the track team, are you?"

"No."

"But you went running? In jeans?"

"It was a spur-of-the-moment thing," I said. I was going to add to the lie, and I knew once I did, I had to keep track of this addition. "I was out for a walk and then this song came on on my phone and it made me want to run. So I ran." I mentally put this information into a folder. Mrs. Cain was nodding at me. I could tell she didn't believe it. But no one could prove it wasn't true. So I'd hold on to it as truth.

"My husband said you were pretty shaken up."

I shrugged. When I didn't say anything else, she sighed and said, "Okay, Rainey. I just wanted to make certain you were okay."

"Can I go?"

"Of course you can go."

I tossed my backpack over a shoulder and walked to the door.

"Oh, Rainey, I forgot to ask."

I stopped.

Turned.

"Yeah?"

"When you and Jordan and Rowan were in here the other day, you didn't happen to borrow a length of black fabric, did you?"

"We didn't borrow anything," I said. "We just helped Jordan with his project."

"Okay."

"Bye." I went into the hallway and finally moved my arms away from my body. I was drenched in sweat. My mind was telling me to do all kinds of things. Hum, whistle, twist, hum, whistle, twitch. I did them all. Luckily the halls were pretty empty, because I was an absolute mess of tics.

I walked home alone, thinking about what an incredible liar I'd become. I wondered if I needed to be lying so much. I mean, what would it matter that we'd been out there filming when that woman crashed her car? We hadn't *made* her do it. At home, Mom didn't seem interested in talking to me. She said a quick hi, then disappeared to do yoga.

I stayed in my room, looking at the videos we'd made. Then I got really paranoid about them, because what if the police *could* charge us with something and demand that I hand over my computer? I made a quick decision and deleted all of them.

But that didn't seem like enough.

I went through my programs, made certain I had backups of everything I needed, then reformatted my computer.

As Windows was reinstalling, Dad came in and sat on the bed. "I heard from Detective Evans," he said.

"Okay."

"The woman in that accident is going to be okay. She had a couple of broken ribs and a concussion."

"Okay."

"She told the police she was out there because she believed she recognized the location of an online video."

I nodded. And kept nodding.

"And she wanted to see if some triangle-headed *thing* lived in the woods there."

"Weird," I said.

"Son, I'm going to ask you this now and then I never will again. Did you have anything to do with that video?"

I kept staring at the install screen. It was at 64 percent. Then 66 percent.

"Son."

"I don't want to say."

"I need you to answer me."

"I need more time. Please give me some more time."

"Son, what kind of trouble are you in?"

"None," I said, fairly certain that was true.

"The woman would like to thank you for being there with her. She said it made her feel safer." He stood from my bed and walked to the door. "You'll feel better when you talk about this."

"I know," I said. "And I will."

Dad left without another word. And I was left with no idea what I should do.

Chapter Ten

There was a new comment on the video the following day. It was long, and I knew as soon as I began to read it that it was written by the woman in the accident.

I have seen this being in my dreams. I call him ChurChaw. I have always wondered if one of my "dreams" wasn't a dream, and I'd actually seen him before and only later did he creep into my dreams. I think I have. I know I have. So when I

saw this video, I knew I had to see him for myself. The thing was, the area looked immediately familiar.

I'd seen those trees before, that bend in the road. I'd seen it a hundred times. It was in an area where my dad used to take us kids fishing in the summer. Then the other night I saw ChurChaw myself. I was so stunned by his presence that I rolled my car and have been in hospital since. My memories are coming back, though, and I feel blessed that I finally witnessed ChurChaw in reality. I now know he is not just a part of my dreams and I will continue to search for him. I know I am not alone with this. There was a boy out there looking for ChurChaw as well. Someone else who must have come face to face with this majestic beast. I would love to talk to you.

I read this three times. ChurChaw! Where did that come from? And the fact that the woman claimed to have seen this thing in her dreams? It was too much to deal with.

“She’s an idiot,” Jordan said at school later that morning. “I told you. A gullible moron.”

“She thought it was some figure from her past. Something she needed to believe was real.”

“Like a moron.” We were walking down the hall on our way to class. “It’s like I said, not our fault she was out there.”

“But it kind of is. If we hadn’t made that video—”

Jordan interrupted me. “If we’d never made the video *and* if she’d never seen it *and* if she hadn’t had messed-up dreams all her life that she believed were true *and* if she hadn’t spent hours figuring out that location *and* if we hadn’t happened to be there again *and* if she hadn’t freaked out and turned too hard *and* if her car hadn’t been going whatever speed it was *and, and, and.* How many of those things were in our control?”

“I guess just the video.”

"We made a video," he said, stopping outside the door to his physics class. "That's all we did. What people decide to do because of that video *they* decide to do." He gave me a pat on the shoulder. "There's nothing the police can charge us with. There's nothing anyone can do. That woman made her choices. We were just there." With that Jordan walked into his class, and I continued down the hall to mine.

I spent the day thinking about this. How much were we to blame? What responsibility did we have when we made a video? It wasn't like we'd given directions to drink bleach or something. It *was* a challenge, but not one that would hurt anyone. We'd only dared people to try to find the thing. That was all. It was just Rowan dressed up. It was just Jordan pulling a prank. It was just me working on my video and marketing skills.

It was just that woman making a whole bunch of decisions because of what she'd seen and what she believed.

But still.

We'd been out there, and that woman would have driven by had Rowan not jumped out of the woods. I didn't even know if he'd seen her car. We didn't *mean* for anything to happen.

That night I looked at the video a few times. It was well done. I knew how it had been made, so I was able to pick out the fake parts. But to the average viewer it would totally look legit. It was a good video, and it had moved around the entire earth. People in China had watched it. South Africa. New Zealand. There were theories about the figure. A whole lore had sprung up around it. The figure was being linked to folk tales in different countries. I could tell some people were writing to try to freak other people out. And there were a ton of people who could tell it was fake and were trying to convince others of this. But that was what we'd set out to do. To create something people would debate. For Jordan it was to prove people are dumb. For Rowan it was because we'd dared him.

But for me it'd been to film and distribute something in a way that made it go viral.

It'd worked.

I'd done my job.

I just wished no one had gotten hurt.

Chapter Eleven

At the end of school the next day, Mrs. Cain held me after class again. She closed the door and sat at her desk, and I stood there before her.

"I've put two and two together," she said. "It really wasn't that difficult. My husband has as well."

"I don't—"

She held a hand up toward me. "Please, don't. I don't mind most things, but I really hate being lied to. I understand why you feel you have to. But I still don't want to hear it."

I said nothing. Mrs. Cain looked out the window, then back at me. "You're going to regret it if you don't go talk to that woman. She needs to know that what she saw out there was fake."

"Why?"

"Because she'll keep searching for it. She'll believe it was real and she'll keep looking."

I thought, And how's this my problem? But I didn't say it.

"You didn't mean for anything bad to happen, but it did. It's not your fault, but it's your responsibility."

I looked away from her. I didn't want to have to discuss any of this. It wasn't my fault, and I didn't think it was my responsibility either.

"My husband, Jeff, is in the parking lot. He says he'll happily take you to the hospital if you'd like to go."

"I don't—"

She interrupted again. "You might not think it's important now, but you will eventually. And you might even regret not taking this opportunity. There's nothing illegal about what happened, but that doesn't mean you can't apologize."

I thought about it a moment longer. "Okay," I said. "I'll go."

"This is the right thing to do," Officer Cain said as we pulled out of the parking lot. I had worried that he'd be in a cruiser and dressed in full uniform. But he was in a minivan with booster seats in the middle row.

"I want to talk to her because I was there, that's all."

"Sure." We drove in silence for a while. "She's a bit on the kooky side," Officer Cain said.

I nodded and shifted in my seat. "She's okay though, right?"

"Physically she'll be okay. A couple of broken ribs, so she'll be sore for a while. Her ankle got messed up and will likely need physio. That kind of stuff. The concussion is worrying. They always are. But she's actually incredibly lucky. It could have been a lot worse."

We drove a while longer in silence. I started to wonder what I was doing. What was I going to say to this woman? It was so awkward, and I wasn't even there yet.

"That's a good video," Officer Cain said. "It looks real. You had me fooled. Not that I thought it was some monster coming out of the woods. But for a second I wondered what was going on. Like, my brain said—maybe... Then I thought, No way."

It was pretty weird getting a play-by-play of Officer Cain's viewing. "So how'd you do it?" he asked.

I looked out the window. We were almost to the hospital.

"I wasn't trying to trick you. Just curious," he said.

"Those videos aren't that hard to do, from what I hear," I said.

"From what you hear. Yeah, okay." We turned into the hospital parking lot and found a spot. "I'll go in with you."

"Like, in the room?" My mind was revving up. I could feel it. Something was going to force its way to the surface soon.

"No, but you'll need to get access. They don't let just anyone visit people."

As we entered I tried to remember when I'd last been in a hospital, but I couldn't. I didn't do anything risky, so I hadn't broken any bones in past years. The halls were mostly empty as we walked through them. Jeff kept talking as we went. Telling me about the different people who were in there. The car accidents, skateboard accidents, accidental stabbings while making dinner. It was a horror show, to be honest.

"Here we are," Officer Cain said, stopping at a door. "Her name's Amanda. She's got a nice cut across her face, so try not to stare at that. And like I said, she's a bit kooky."

"What am I supposed to do?"

"Talk to her. She wants to thank you for what you did that night." He pulled the door handle down but didn't open the door. "A bit ironic, isn't it?"

The room was dim. The woman, Amanda, turned as soon as I stepped in.

"I know you," she said. She rose up slightly in her bed. "You were there that night. You were the boy."

"I was," I said. "How are you?"

"I'll be okay," she said. "Have a seat."

She looked really excited to see me. It felt weird.

"So you know ChurChaw?"

"I—"

"I've been remembering. Remembering a lot. I didn't first see him in a dream. I saw him for real. Have you seen him for real?"

"I–

"I was ten. Sorry to interrupt, but I have been waiting for someone to talk to. Someone who understands. I was ten, and we were camping. I'm an only child. Are you an only child?"

"Yes–" I managed before being interrupted again.

"Maybe he only comes for children. I don't know. But we were camping, and I had to go pee. It was the middle of the night."

She turned and looked at the blinds covering the window as if she could see outside. It was weird to hear this woman talk about having to pee.

"I didn't see anything on the way there. It was bright. One of those nights where the moon is high and there aren't any clouds. So the trees and the branches and everything were casting shadows.

I think that would scare some people, but for me it was so much fun. I loved being out there where it was so quiet." She turned to me. "What's your name?"

"Rainey," I said.

"I like that. Like a rainy day."

She kept looking at me. I was about to say, "Yeah," but she went on.

"I had my pee. You know, in the outhouse-type thing. There are always lots of spiders and stuff in there. That I don't like, but if you don't bother them, they won't bother you. So I'm walking back to the campsite, and I take a wrong turn. Did you say you go camping?"

"I've been."

"So you know those twisty trails. You sometimes end up walking right into someone's site. I got on the wrong trail, though, and when I figured it out, I turned around and there he was." She smiled at me.

"ChurChaw?"

"ChurChaw. I named him that right then. He gave me the name by making this noise—*churrrr chawwwww*. And you'd think I'd have been scared. All alone in the woods like that. But I wasn't. He wasn't threatening or anything. He just stood there and made that sound. *Churrr chawwwww*. His head, the big triangle thing, it moved back and forth. When I stepped toward him, he disappeared. But the thing was, I felt so at peace in that moment. Unlike I'd ever felt before. I wasn't a troubled child or anything, but I often had...not voices, but conversations in my head. They'd come out of nowhere and were about nothing in particular a lot of the time. But they were there. And in that moment, I had the feeling I wouldn't have that anymore, and I haven't. Can you believe it?"

"Yeah," I said. "Sure."

"What's your story? What's your connection to ChurChaw?"

I thought about it. Amanda stared at me. She looked so hopeful.

"The thing is," I said, "what you saw out there wasn't real. I don't mean when you were ten. I mean the video. I made that."

"Sorry?"

"We were doing this thing. To get a viral video, really. Seeing how far it would go. Me and two of my friends made it and put it online. When you ran off the road the other night, we were out doing another shoot. But what you saw was just a guy in a costume with a foam triangle on his head." It sounded so stupid to say it all out loud.

"No," she said. "It was him."

Even in the darkness of the room, I could see she'd gone a paler white.

"I'm not saying what you saw when you were a kid wasn't real. It totally could have been. But we came up with that costume and—"

"Get out."

"Sorry?"

"Get out. If you're going to lie to me. I have enough people lying to me. You can leave."

"I'm sorry," I said.

"For what?"

"For what happened."

"You had nothing to do with it."

I stood and walked to the door. "I am sorry though. I hope you get better soon."

Amanda had turned away from me. I couldn't be certain, but I thought she might have been crying.

Chapter Twelve

I came clean that night.

It wasn't easy.

I'd lied to my parents, and I didn't know if they'd ever look at me the same way again. I mean, I know parents *know* their kids lie to them. But they expect little white lies. Nothing this big.

"I didn't want to say who was out there with me," I told Dad once I'd said the whole thing.

"Who was it?"

"Jordan Hawley and this guy Rowan."

"The Hawley kid." He tilted his head. "I can see that."

"We never meant for anything to happen. We wanted to make a video that would go viral. It was really to see how to do it. To make it work."

"And it did."

We were in the living room. Mom was out for book club.

"It did. I didn't mean for that woman to get hurt. But she's going to be okay."

"Physically," Dad said. "Not likely mentally." He let that sit. "Your mom's brother, your uncle Henry. He had a car accident when he was twenty-two. A bad one. He's never driven again and is, well, you know, a bit of a shut-in." I must have looked worried because Dad went on. "I'm not saying that this Amanda woman will have the same issues. Not at all. But just because your body heals doesn't mean your mind will."

I had been sensing a tic coming on since I'd sat down with Dad. It wasn't that I ticced out whenever I got nervous, but being nervous certainly didn't help.

"I know," I said. "I guess we didn't think of that."

"Who could? Right? I want you to remember that you're a good kid. You meant no one any harm. What you did was potentially dangerous. But at the same time, everyone has to take responsibility for their own actions."

"Yeah," I said. "I've been through all this in my head already."

"I imagine you have." Dad stood up. "I'm about to go out. I'm disappointed in you for lying. But I understand. Rainey, please know that you can tell us the truth. Always."

"I do, but the police—"

"I know. I get it."

I whistled and twisted my head three times and then felt better.

"You okay here?"

"Yeah."

Dad put on his coat and opened the front door. Before he stepped out he said, "Don't be too hard on yourself, son."

I nodded and felt like I was going to cry. I'd never thought my parents would get *really* angry with me about this. But I'd had no idea they would be so fine with it either.

When the house was quiet I went up to my room. I'd lost a lot of stuff when I wiped my computer. I'd thought I had backed it all up and could likely find most of it on one cloud or another, but I started to think maybe it was better to begin again. Start something new. I'd learned a lot with the fight and figure videos. I mean, I was no great film director or anything, but it had been a start.

I dug through the videos I had on one cloud server. I'd filmed a lot before. There were endless shots of people in parks, out by the river, even in school hallways. I started meshing them together for no real reason and then brought some CGI into play. Explosions, reptile heads replacing real heads, people talking in different voices. It was so easy.

I went back to the figure video. It was still gaining more views. I wondered how long it would go on like that. Someone had put a link in the comments to a site I didn't recognize, but it seemed legit enough to click on.

The site was one of those ones that investigate fakes. It was really just a cluttered page filled with videos. The first one I clicked on had an actor saying something about another actor. He was laughing as he spoke. But his voice didn't sound quite right. It was close, but not exactly right. Someone had posted that it had to be a deep fake, but they hadn't been able to tell how it had been done or be certain. I downloaded the video and looked at the properties. Everything had been stripped, which was a good sign it wasn't real. I moved through the video in super slow motion, looking at every frame. It all looked really legit until it didn't.

The actor's head turned to one side, and there was a stitch there. A space where you could tell the video had been altered. There were two faces, almost as though one was wearing a mask and it had slipped.

I took a screenshot and then advanced further. Four other spots weren't right. It was a two-minute video. I collected the pictures and posted them under the video. **Proof. This is fake.**

I looked at the clock on my computer. I'd been staring at that video for over an hour.

The responses came in quickly.

Thank you. I knew it.

Reposted to social media. Thanks.

Awesome. CNN posted this. Going to look sooooo dumb.

I had no idea the video was already out there. And it seemed fairly easy for me to find the seams. You just had to look closely. And know what to look for.

My computer binged. I looked at the page and found I had a message.

Hey, good work. Can you look at this one? I can't figure out where it's been edited. There was a video attached. It showed a politician. He sounded okay, and he looked okay, but after a minute I could tell something had been edited. There was a stutter in one word. The video clicked a couple of times. This is fun, I thought. And could actually be useful.

Acknowledgments

A huge thank you to everyone at Orca. Although I know everyone there does an amazing job, I'd like to single out two people this time: Tanya Trafford and Vivian Sinclair. I could go through a manuscript a hundred times and still not catch everything you two do.

orca soundings

NOW WHAT? Read on for an excerpt from *Shark*

Mark is good at pool, *really* good. But others want to take advantage of his natural talent, whether Mark is willing or not.

→

Chapter One

The place was called Minnesota's, a cavernous room beneath a strip mall full of respectable suburban shops. The sign outside continued to inform that Halloween was upon us, even though it was the end of February. Inside, rows of pool tables ran the length of the room, buffered from the walls by pinball and vintage video-game machines. The soundtrack was classic rock, balls clacking off one another and bursts of excited cheering. The fragrance: spilled beer and cigarettes smoked a decade before.

It felt, in every way possible, like home.

I found Minnesota's when my mom, sister and I moved here a month ago. The regulars were cool and always looking for a game. The owner was happy to give the odd free ginger ale when I'd been there a while. But best of all, there was absolutely no betting permitted.

I had sunk the three and the five when I noticed this guy watching me from a couple of tables away. He was tall, thickset, with an unruly mess of hair on his head and an equally untamed beard on his face. I'd never seen him before. His clothes screamed biker—the leather vest over printed T, extremely blue jeans cinched up with an extra-large buckled, studded belt.

"Am I going to get to play this game?"

I looked across the table at Hippy. He was tall and thin, dropped into a vintage Pearl Jam shirt and cargo pants. Sandals over thick socks in the dead of winter. He was the day manager but always found time for a couple of games.

The one and the four were left on the table for me. Plus the eight ball, of course. The one was an easy shot. The four, way more difficult. I was challenging myself to not take the easy shot. I lined up the four, and Hippy clicked his tongue. He did this every time he saw an easier shot available. I figured he'd catch on to what I was doing someday.

The four bounced off the edge of the corner pocket and sat there spinning.

"Yes," Hippy said. "I shall now destroy you." He pulled his long hair from his face and leaned over the table.

I sat on a high stool and, pretending to watch Hippy take his shot, glanced over at the biker guy. He'd gone back to playing alone on one of the large snooker tables.

"Come on fifteen, don't be cruel," Hippy said, leaning low to the table. It looked like he was attempting to send the ball into a pocket by sheer force of will. But the fifteen just sat there, right on the cusp of the pocket. Hippy stood to his full height and rubbed his stubbled chin. "All right, Shark, finish me off."

I leaned over the table and focused on the four, which was now an easy shot. Or, at least, no more difficult than the one.

"Shark?" I looked up to find the biker guy at the end of the table, looking right at me.

"It's just a nickname," I said. I didn't want to get into the whole thing. My name's Mark, but when I was younger my little sister put an S on the front of a lot of her words, and so to my family I became Shark. I'd told Hippy this story one day and instantly regretted it.

"Looks earned to me," biker guy said.

"Hippy," a waitress called from behind the bar. "That thing's backed up again."

Hippy shook his head and set his cue into the wall rack. "You play him, War," Hippy said. "I have to take care of this."

"War?" I said.

"Nickname," the biker guy said. "Name's Warren." He stepped forward and extended a hand. I shook it, then got low to the table again to finish the game Hippy and I had been playing.

I wasn't sure I wanted to play War that evening. The whole feeling of the pool hall changed for me the instant Hippy walked away. Everything got heavy, if that's a way to describe it. I don't know—I've never been that good with words.

"Good to meet you," I said.

I finished the game easily. The one and four found pockets, and after bouncing the cue off two bumpers, I sank the eight.

War began racking the balls into the triangle. "Where'd you learn to play?" he asked.

I sat on the high stool again and took a sip from the ginger ale I'd been working on.

"My dad," I said, leaving it at that.

"Basement table?" He wiggled the balls in the triangle until they were tight, then slowly lifted the frame off the table.

"Mostly pool halls," I said.

War picked up his cue. "So," he said, leaning down to set his aim on the cue ball. "Where's dad now?"

"Not around," I said. War was drawing his cue back and forth. It was my table though. Whenever you win a game, you own the table. If someone wants to play you, they have to let you break. It's etiquette, but the kind of etiquette that is pretty much a rule.

He hammered the cue ball into the triangle of balls. I watched as they spread out across the table. The fifteen and twelve dropped, but the cue ball settled in right behind the three. In eight-ball, you're either low ball or high. That means you either have to get balls one through seven in, or the nine through fifteen. And then, of course, to finish it off, the eight. When you break and sink a couple of balls, you have the advantage of taking a follow-up shot to decide whether it's the low or high end you need to play.

"That's too bad," War said. I thought he was talking about where the cue ball was sitting, but then he continued. "My dad ditched when I was twelve." I let him take his shot. He decided against the four, which was perfectly lined up, hoping, it seemed, to get the eleven in and play the high balls. Instead, he tapped the eleven into the perfect position for me to sink it.

"You're low ball," I said. I didn't want to talk about my dad. I went to pool halls to feel close to him. Playing pool was the one thing we had done together that hadn't ended badly. It was the time I had felt most connected to my dad. But that was all in the past, and if I've learned anything, it's that it's best to leave it there.

The remaining high balls were in perfect positions for me to run the table. Which was exactly what I did. I didn't feel the need to hold back.

"Nicely done," War said when I'd finished. "Another?"

I checked my phone. Almost seven already. "Not tonight," I said. "I have to go." I shrugged into my jacket.

War came over to shake my hand. "That was a hell of a game," he said.

"Thanks." I shook his hand. "Maybe play again sometime?"

He let go of my hand. "Sounds good," he said with a smile. "I'll be here practicing."

His smile felt genuine. It seemed kind. It lit up his face in a way that reminded me of the only nice teacher I'd ever had.

Jeff Ross is the author of many novels for young adults, including several titles in the Orca Soundings and Orca Sports series. He teaches scriptwriting and English at Algonquin College in Ottawa.

orca soundings

For more information on all the books

in the Orca Soundings line, please visit

orcabook.com